Christopher Columbus
(Cristóbal Colón)

Plate 1

Diego Columbus (Colón)
(son of Columbus and Felipa)

Felipa Perestrello e Moniz
(wife of Columbus)

Plate 2

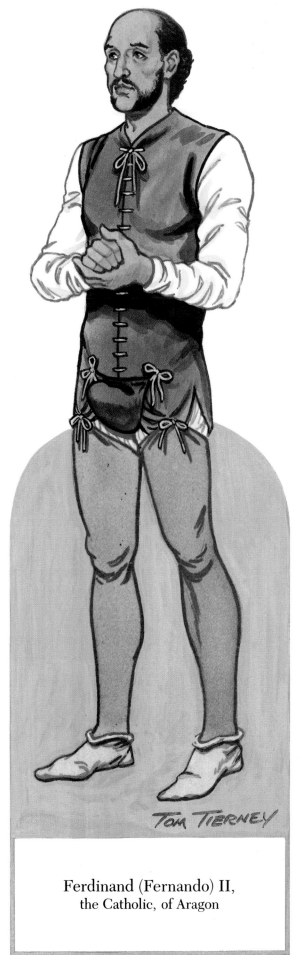

Isabella (Isabel) I,
the Catholic, of Castile

Ferdinand (Fernando) II,
the Catholic, of Aragon

Plate 3

Beatriz Enríquez

Hernando Columbus (Colón)
(son of Columbus and Beatriz)

Plate 4

Vicente Yáñez Pinzón
(commander of the *Niña*)

Martín Alonso Pinzón
(brother of Vicente and
commander of the *Pinta*)

Plate 5

Columbus and Diego as
vagabonds

Plate 6

Columbus as an academician

Plate 7

Isabella and Ferdinand in
royal robes

Plate 8

CC

D

D

do not cut
out white area
near right wrist

Columbus as a wealthy merchant

Diego as a court page

Plate 9

do not cut out area near right wrist

D

FP

Diego as a courtier

Felipa in a rich gown

Plate 10

Beatriz in fine clothing

Hernando in court garb

Plate 11

Vicente and Martín Pinzón
dressed for the flag-planting
ceremonies on San Salvador

Plate 12

Columbus claiming San Salvador
for Spain

Plate 13

Isabella and Ferdinand greeting
Columbus after his first voyage

Plate 14

Columbus dressed as a
Franciscan monk after his
second voyage

Columbus brought back in chains
after his third voyage

Plate 15